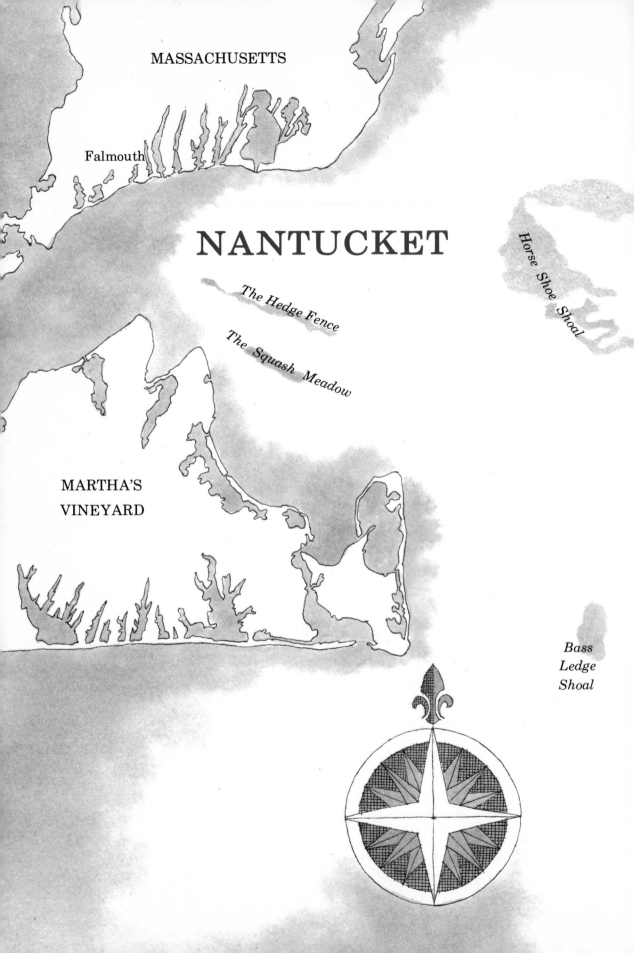

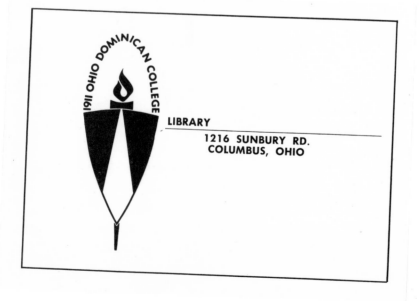

ZENAS *and the*
SHAVING MILL

by F. N. MONJO

illustrations by Richard Cuffari

Coward, McCann & Geoghegan, Inc.

New York

*Halfmoon
Shoal*

*Cross Rip
Shoal*

SOUND

Tuckernuck Shoal

THE
BAR

NANTUCKET

A T L A N T I C   O C E A N

Acknowledgments

For their assistance in helping me prepare this book, I should particularly like to thank Miss Barbara Andrews, Librarian, and Miss Janice Williams, Assistant Librarian, of the Nantucket Atheneum, for their kindness in helping me find printed versions of Keziah Coffin Fanning's *Diary,* for telling me the pronunciation of Keziah's name (Ke-zī'-ah) and many other helpful hints of information.

F.N.M.

Text copyright © 1976 by F. N. Monjo
Illustrations copyright © 1976 by Richard Cuffari
Published simultaneously in Canada by
Longman Canada Limited, Toronto.

Library of Congress Cataloging in Publication Data
Monjo, F. N.
Zenas and the shaving mill.
SUMMARY: A young Quaker boy relates how he eludes the
ships of both the British and the rebels while sailing to
Nantucket with supplies.
[1. United States—History—Revolution, 1775-1783—
Fiction. 2. Friends, Society of—Fiction] I. Cuffari,
Richard, 1925-   II. Title.
PZ7.M75Ze3   [Fic]   75-32531
ISBN 0-698-20326-7
ISBN 0-698-30579-5

PRINTED IN THE UNITED STATES OF AMERICA

Contents

for Sirkka, Christina, Rolf, and John

Chapter One:
SAILING OUT OF FALMOUTH

I'm sailing east from Falmouth,
sailing for the island.
The wind is nearly dead ahead, against me.
And the clouds look kind of squally.
It's what we call a two-reef breeze
on Nantucket, where I come from.
And when one of them two-reefers blows up,
we take in sail and we double-reef accordin'.

Since the wind is east and I must beat out against it,
I'm short-reaching, back and forth,
tacking as careful as can be,

trying to get back home to Nantucket
before night closes in.
I'm fetching a load of wood and flour
and other sundries for Mother.
"Zenas," said Mother, "whatever thee does,
be sure to find me some onions.
And don't forget the potatoes."

To look about thee, thee might suppose
that my sloop, the *Lively Abby*, and I
had the whole wide ocean to play about in.
But that would be thy great mistake.
For 'twixt Falmouth and Nantucket,
where thee finds me, there is
but one deep channel of water to sail in,
like a long narrow corridor, in Nantucket Sound.
And on either side of the channel
there's tide rips, where the water boils.
And shallow places . . .
shoals where the breakers roar and foam.
And many a sunken wreck that could tell thee
sad tales of how they got lost in the fog.
And ran aground on hidden sands
and were dashed apart by the waves.

Passing the island of Martha's Vineyard,
I'm leaving to port a long, long shoal
that we islanders call "The Hedge Fence."

8

And off to starboard,
half a mile hence,
is another round shoal we call "The Squash Meadow."
And after I've left them both astern,
the *Lively Abby* and I
will skim between Horseshoe and Tuckernuck shoals.
We'll run south for Nantucket
and try to creep over the harbor bar
before anyone can stop us.

Now, if thee would understand my story,
thee must mind every word that I say
explaining the tide rips, the shoals, and the bar.
For as luck would have it,
in order to enter Nantucket harbor,
you must sail over a great sunken sandbar,
stretched clear across the harbor mouth.

And thee can't cross over it anytime safe
excepting at high tide.
And even then thee must know thy way
if thee would not run aground.
For even though Nantucket lies
full thirty miles out in the open sea—
out of sight of the mainland,
in the midst of the wide, wide ocean—
still, there's hidden shoals all around it.
Shoals lying fifteen miles out at sea,

waiting to catch an unwary vessel
and crush its hull like a walnut shell.
There's the Rose and Crown
way out to the east.
And Handkerchief Shoal to the north.
And the Bishop and Clerks,
and Bass Ledge, and Cross Rip,
and Half-Moon Shoal,
and Shovelful Shoal,
and Old Man Shoal,
and a dozen more I could name thee—
and guide thee past in safety too!
For ain't I Zenas Coffin?
And ain't I sailed these dangerous waters
a good ten years or more?
And ain't I a man of experience,
a full seventeen years old?
If it weren't for the war that's rumbling now,
I'd have been at sea
a good two years past, I can tell thee.
I'd have sailed off, hunting for whales,
to Brazil and to Greenland, I would.
'Stead of fetching potatoes and onions from Falmouth
for Mother and Sister Jedidah.

Some four years back, let me tell thee,
my grandfather, Benjamin Coffin,
he says to my father, "Micajah," says he,

"as soon as thee sends thy son, Zenas, to sea,
the better for Zenas, for thee, and for me!
For I can't do a *particle* with that boy!"
Now, that's what Grandfather said.
And Grandfather teaches school in Nantucket—
though everyone else 'cept him named Coffin
been off huntin' whales these last sixty years.
But not Grandfather. He's a teacher,
and he's been trying to learn me
spelling and figures and Latin.
But I just ain't no scholar.
"Micajah, I tell thee," says he to Father,
"there's no whacking Latin into that boy!
And precious little English, for the matter of that!
I can't pound in the one nor t'other."
So Father just gives me one of them grins
and he says, "Well, Zenas, we'll send thee to sea."
And that's where thee'd found me,
a good two years since,
if it wasn't for all of them waging this war.

Chapter Two:
WHAT DOES THEE THINK OF THAT?

If thee but knew it, this war may be thought
to have begun right here on Nantucket.
Two of our ships sailed out from here—
the *Dartmouth* and the *Beaver*—
owned by our richest merchant and whaler,
Master William Rotch.
They sailed to London, full of whale oil.
And there the British filled them with tea
and sent them back to Boston.
Once they got there, the Liberty Boys
dressed up like Indians
and threw that cargo of tea into the bay.

Fighting about some tax, they were,
and they called it the Boston Tea Party.
Don't expect *me* to explain it!
But that, as I've told thee, was
when the war began—when they spoiled the tea
in Master Rotch's vessels.
And Boston sent word to us here on Nantucket
that *we* must go to war, too.

The Liberty Boys in Massachusetts
said we must fight for them.
And the British over in London
said that we were expected
to do the very same for them.
Though how they expected us to
fight for *both* sides
is more than I can tell.
Most of us Friends,
out here on Nantucket,
didn't want to fight for one nor t'other.
And what does thee think of that?
We're Friends, or Quakers,
the most of us here.
We say "thee" and "thou,"
and we never wear
gay colors to our clothes.
We don't allow our portraits painted
or pictures of any kind in our homes.

And we don't have churchbells or music or dancing.
We don't swear oaths, and we don't bow down.
And we don't take our hats off for any man living.
For ain't I as good as thee?
And we don't take up arms and go to war.
For how should I kill thee, my fellowman,
when I know thy life is as sweet to thee
as mine is dear to me?

But when two sides start in
to fight them a war,
it's no use for a little island like us
to try to stay peaceable betwixt 'em.
Both sides came after us hard, to come in,
and we tried to stay clear of 'em both.
We'd like to be friendly to everybody,
but all we got for our pains, so far,
is to make both sides
just as angry as hornets.
For the Liberty Boys don't trust us. They hate us.
And the British in London feel just the same
and hate us like poison, too.

If we try to send any of our ships out to sea,
whaling or fishing
(and what else would a Nantucketer know how to do?),
here come the British, with all of their navy,
to seize our ships, send our sailors to prison,

and to steal our fish and our barrels of whale oil.
And most of our ships that ain't took by the British
are took by the Liberty Boys.

We Friends won't put cannons or guns on our ships,
for we don't believe in fighting.
And there's not enough farmland on our island
to feed the half of us proper.
Now, if we can't fish
and can't hardly farm,
we'll most of us end up starving or freezing
before this war is over.
There's not enough food or wood on Nantucket
to keep us alive through this winter.
Unless we fight for the Liberty Boys,
they won't supply us with nothing from the mainland.
And the British won't let us go fishing or whaling
unless we fight for *them*.
Both of them trying to force us to fight.
But we Friends won't fight for either!
That's why I'm here, in the *Lively Abby*,
smuggling food for Mother.
Trying to get home before somebody stops me.
Trying to run in over the bar
with my sacks of potatoes and onions
before I get caught.
And here comes a sail moving up fast behind me!
There's cannon on deck, and she's chasing me hard!

20

So I must race for the bar, at the harbor . . .
She sails faster than me, and she'll catch me
unless I can lead her into the shoals
and run her aground, maybe.
I've no guns, and she has cannon.
Now, what does thee think of that?

Chapter Three:
IN TIME OF WAR

Does thee know what happens in time of war
when thee's caught betwixt two sides fighting?
Here's what happened to William Rotch,
our richest whale-oil merchant.
He's a Friend, of course,
and him and a party of Friends—male and female—
sailed from here across Nantucket Sound
to Cape Cod to attend the Quaker meeting
held at Sandwich last summer.
Well, wouldn't thee guess their ship was taken?
Stopped by an American privateer
(or a "shaving mill," as we sometimes call 'em).

A privateer is a ship, with cannon,
carrying papers signed by the Liberty Boys
saying it's lawful to chase and capture
any peaceful merchant ship they can.
Well, William Rotch and everyone with him
had all their money and watches took.
They figured they'd lost their ship as well,
and all of them thought they was going to prison . . .
when up sails a British man-of-war
and captures the American privateer!
And the British captain
set all the Nantucketers free!
So William Rotch and the rest of the Friends
come safe home after all.
They were lucky, of course.
And so was my father, Micajah.
He sailed off to Philadelphia
to fetch home a cargo of flour in barrels.
On his way home the British caught him,
captured his ship,
and carried him prisoner to New York.
He managed to get back safe to Nantucket
after he talked them into letting him go.
But he lost his ship forever.
So Father just got him another vessel
and sailed off in her once again.
He knew we'd starve if he didn't.
I'm worried he may not be so lucky always

if he keeps on making these voyages.
But there's none of us safe
ashore on our island.
For both sides keep raiding
to steal what we got—
and that's little enough, as I said.

The Liberty Boys from Massachusetts
stole fifty whale boats right out of our harbor!
Their shaving mills—that's their privateers—
sail into port here whenever they like.
Arresting Tories, taking them prisoner,
breaking in houses and stores and such.
Carrying off beds and tables and food
and anything else they can lay their hands on.
How can we stop them? They got guns,
and we don't believe in shooting. . . .
That's why we call them "shaving mills,"
'cause they shave us clean of everything we own.
Not long ago the British and their Tory friends
sailed out to Martha's Vineyard,
took off all of their sheep and cows,
and took all their money, too.
We heard they was planning to raid *us* next
and do the same to Nantucket.
So we hid our sheep and our cows in the swamp.
We buried our money.
What little food we had left

we carted out of town and hid it
wherever we could.
(I even heard that Shabael Macy
hid his daughter, Bethiah,
under a heap of flax in his barn,
so's the British sailors couldn't never find her.
Now, I don't know if the story's *true*.
But I do know Bethiah ain't all that pretty.)

Well, every day we expected the worst.
Expected the British to sail from the Vineyard.
We watched and we waited, but they never came.
Seems the wind blew steady against them that week,
till they gave up hope of the venture.
And we was saved, *that* time.

But whenever a British man-of-war
comes upon a Nantucket whaler or fishing boat
out on the high seas, he'll give her a chase.
And alack-a-day! if he should catch her.
For he'll put every man aboard in irons.
Now, after four years of that kind of fighting,
we've lost most of our fleet of ships to the British,
and most of our sailors are clapped in jail.

The British men-of-war
and the American shaving mills
chase any merchant ship they see—

not just Quaker ships from Nantucket.
Many get caught, and some get away,
and some merchantmen run aground
on the shoals of Nantucket.
Then we row out and take off the sailors
and help them save their cargoes.

Tories or British or Liberty Boys—
whoever sails into our harbor with guns—
all of them know we're Friends.
And all of them know we're defenseless.
They know we got *nothing* to fight them with.
So wouldn't thee think they'd be ashamed
to treat us as they do?
They come right in and take everything we got,
'less we hide it or bury it or carry it off.

One time some shaving mills armed with cannon
sailed right into our harbor.
They was full of Tories, and they
started looting the town.
They posted sentries with guns and bayonets
in all our streets, and they told
all the folks to stay in their houses.
Wouldn't even let people come out into the square
to fetch drinking water from the town pump.
Well, Deborah Chase,
she wanted some water

to make a fish chowder for supper.
And Deborah, she's a gigantic big girl,
and people don't trifle with her,
for she's mighty strong, I can tell thee.
Strong enough to overturn a cart in the street,
for haven't I seen her *do* it?
And isn't her brother, Reuben, a sailor,
in John Paul Jones' ship, *Ranger*?

Her father said, "Daughter, I bid thee stay home,
or thee'll have a bayonet in thee."
But Deborah wanted that water real bad for her chowder,
and she was determined to have it.
So she hooked two buckets—two big iron-bound buckets—
onto a yolk and went hulking out into the square.
She tramped right up to the pump, she did,
and the Tory sentry says, "Halt!"
Deborah just grabs the pump handle,
like she never heard him at all,
and when the sentry pokes his bayonet at her,
she swings her bucket, hard as she can,
and larrups him over the head with a *thump!*
And he falls out flat, on the cobblestones,
for she'd knocked that sentry senseless.
Then she draws her water, tramps back home,
and fixes a nice hot fish chowder.
As I said, all us Friends are peaceable folk.
But that don't mean we're cowards!

Chapter Four:
MY AUNT KEZIAH

Aunt Keziah Coffin keeps a grocery store,
but she don't have much to sell in it these days.
Folks say she's a Tory and sides with the British.
They say she's a smuggler and runs in
flour and potatoes and cornmeal and such
by night from Long Island.
And they say she charges terrible high prices
just because there's a war on.
I expect some of what they say is true,
but I don't know how much.

One time a British man-of-war

lay off Nantucket harbor bar.
He was mounting thirty-two cannon,
and the British admiral in command
had his wife on board.
Well, he sent in to town for some groceries.
Aunt Keziah sent his wife some turnips
and butter and eggs and marmalade and cheese.
Sent her some cranberries, too.
Whole town was furious with her for doing it.
"Zenas," says my Aunt Keziah,
"if I hadn't sent that woman those supplies,
that ship could have blowed this town flat
in an hour. Blowed it flat with them cannon!"
Folks say she was wrong to do what she did,
being a Quaker Friend, against war,
yet helping it along, like she done,
with eggs and cheese and marmalade.
But it ain't so easy to stay out of this war,
with both sides trying to push thee in!
And it's hard to be good if thee's just a bit stingy
and fond of money like my Aunt Keziah.
It's hard if thee's just a little bit "near,"
as we say of such folk on Nantucket.

My cousin Keziah, Aunt Keziah's daughter,
is keeping a diary about all that happens.
She wanted to marry a man from Long Island,
did my cousin Keziah. His name's Fanning.

Phineas Fanning. And he's one of them
that shipped in supplies to Aunt Keziah's grocery.
He'd sail over from Long Island by night,
dodging British men-of-war
and Liberty Boys' shaving mills both.
So the Liberty Boys called him a Tory.
And the British called him a rebel.
But we hungry folk on Nantucket was grateful,
and we just called him our friend.

Now, Phineas Fanning ain't a *Quaker* Friend,
but he's a friend just the same,
if thee understands me.
My cousin Keziah fell in love with him,
and he asked her to marry.
He was a Presbyterian, and some of our Quaker ladies
come to visit cousin Keziah.
They told her she couldn't keep coming
to Quaker meeting if she kept on
wearing silks and frills like she did.
Nor could she be counted a Friend no more
if she went and married Fanning.
Does thee know what cousin Keziah done?
Despite what them Quaker ladies said?
She went and married Phineas Fanning.
And she kept on wearing her frills.
I'd never let no ladies tell *me* who to marry,
would thee?

Folks say Aunt Keziah is a Tory,
selling flour and stuff to the British.
And so the Liberty Boys from Massachusetts
come over here and carried her off to Cape Cod
and put her on trial. They called her a smuggler.
But Aunt Keziah proved to them
that her store was broke into and looted
by *both* sides during the war.
She said it so tart they let her off scot-free!

And now does thee see what I mean
when I tell thee it's hard to be peaceable?
With both sides pushing thee into a war?

Chapter Five:
THE SHAVING MILL

I named this sloop the *Lively Abby*.
Named her after my sweetheart, Abial—
Abial Gardner, the girl that I'll marry
as soon as this war's at an end.
Both the girl and the sloop
are just as trim and as pretty
as thee could wish them to be.

My sloop is so long and so fast and so narrow
she skims over the shoals
as light as if she were a gull or a tern.
Whenever I go to the mainland

for cornmeal or flour or salt pork,
it's the *Lively Abby* brings me safe home.
And if ever I'm chased by a shaving mill,
Lively Abby takes wing and leaves her astern.
That's why I ain't all that worried about that shaving mill
that's following after me now!

We don't have half enough firewood out on the island.
Even when we cut peat in the swamps
and chop up the scrub oaks, roots and all.
We'll have little to burn
and little to eat
till this war is brought to an end.
And all of us sailors can set out to sea,
fishing for codfish and whales.
Now, Horseshoe Shoal lies ahead and to port.
And that shaving mill's coming up fast!
Booming along, trying to take me.
She's got cannon on board,
but she draws little water.
Her sails are billowing and she's faster than me.

But there's a Yankee-good chance
I can run her aground on the Horseshoe Shoal
and just leave her stuck there, high and dry,
for the next six hours or more,
till the next high tide sets her free.
Then I'll skim over Nantucket bar

and have all this food hid safe in my cellar
before that shaving mill can scrape free
and float herself off of the shoal!

That's why I'm taking this long reach to port.
Dodging right through the shallowest ground.
She may be a Tory or a Liberty Boy.
I don't know, and I don't care.
I can't let her catch me, whichever she is.
If I can just hang her up somewhere,
here on the Horseshoe,
she'll be fouled in the sands, and I shall go free!
I'm over the shallowest part of the shoal now,
and the shaving mill's pressing me hard!
There's eight men aboard her with two swivel guns,
both of them pointing at me!
I keep reaching to port. They keep plowing onward.
Now, look there! There's a jolt!
They've run on the sandbar! Her rail is awash!
And eight men are hip-deep in the foam!
They're cursing and calling!
But I'm out of gunshot.
And they're stuck on the Horseshoe
for hours to come!

Now all I must do is set sail for the harbor
and let the *Lively Abby* carry me home
with this pork and potatoes and onions for chowder,
or whatever Mother may fancy to serve.

So I'll talk to the gulls and the terns
as I'm sailing.
I'll think of Abial, the girl that I'll marry.
I'll creep over the bar and make my sloop safe.
I'll count up the whales I'll hunt at war's close.
I'll pray for Father and all of the rest still at sea—
for when *they'll* get home,
the good Lord alone knows.

ABOUT THIS STORY

No attempt has been made to put the events of this story in chronological order, but everything related here did indeed occur in Nantucket during the American Revolution (1776–83). The islanders (most of whom were Quakers) were for the most part nonviolent and therefore wanted to ally themselves with neither side. But they were harassed by Tory patriots who had left Nantucket to join the British, by men-of-war of the regular British navy, and by raiding parties of Liberty Boys from the Massachusetts coast.

Since neither the Americans nor the British wanted to supply them with food, the Nantucketers continually suffered from lack of supplies—flour, potatoes, meat, vegetables, and firewood—and their sailors and vessels were captured by combatants on both sides.

William Rotch, Deborah Chase, Keziah Coffin, and Zenas Coffin all lived at the time of this story.

Will Gardner, author of *The Coffin Saga*, has written that "Zenas slipped in and out of Nantucket, eluding his pursuers; more than one 'shaving mill' [privateer] sailed by a British skipper or a colonist refugee [Tory] seeking to enrich himself found himself aground on the bar because Zenas had led him into shallow places."

Six years after the Revolution ended, in 1789, Zenas Coffin shipped aboard Captain Benjamin Hussey's whaler, *Greyhound.* Later he married Abial Gardner, by whom he had three boys and three girls. Before he was thirty he was captain of his own whaleship. And when he died, in 1828, he was a wealthy man, owning seven whaleships and 150,000 barrels of whale oil.